William and the ghost

'On Monday,' said Mrs Patel, 'we are going to visit Gloomy Castle.'

'Great!' said Hamid. 'I like castles. I hope it has a ghost or two.'

'I don't think it's great,' groaned William. 'It means we'll miss swimming. There are no such things as ghosts, anyway.'

'We shall have to plan our visit carefully,' said Mrs Patel, 'so I'm going to hand out some work sheets about the Castle.'

William looked at the picture of Gloomy Castle that
Mrs Patel had drawn. It had towers, battlements,
and a moat. On the other work sheets there were
things to do and things to find out.

'Oh no!' groaned William. 'Why do we have to go
on a swimming day? This place looks really boring.
I'll bet it's full of old junk.'

'We'll be going on a coach,' said Hamid. 'I love
going on coaches wherever they go!'

'It won't be as much fun as swimming,' said William.

'Well, I'm looking forward to it,' laughed Hamid.
'I'm going to enjoy myself, and you will, too.'

2

That evening William told his sister, Julie, about the visit to Gloomy Castle.

'You'll love it,' she said. 'It's a very old, creepy, sort of place. It's supposed to have a ghost, and secret rooms, and lost treasure. I have a booklet about it upstairs. Do you want me to find it for you?'

'I suppose so,' said William, 'but I don't know why we have to miss swimming.'

William began to read the booklet Julie gave him. He was soon very interested in the story of the old house. Long, long ago the Earl of Gloomy had made the King very angry. The Earl disappeared and so did all his treasure. They were never seen again.

On Monday the class went by coach to Gloomy Castle.

'What a fantastic place!' said Hamid. 'It can't have changed a bit for ages and ages. I wonder what it was like when people rode horses and wore funny clothes and hats and boots.'

'I expect they'd think our clothes were pretty funny,' said William.

'Now before we go in to Gloomy Castle,' said Mrs Patel, 'I want you all to listen to Mr Carter. He is the guide, and will answer any questions you want to ask.'

'The first building here was a monastery,' said Mr
Carter. 'A monastery is a place where monks live.'

'Did he say monkeys?' whispered William.

'Monks,' said Hamid. Mrs Patel frowned at them.

'When the monastery was pulled down, Gloomy Castle
was built in its place,' explained Mr Carter.
At question time William asked about the Earl's
treasure. He wanted to know if the story was true.

'Ah, so you know that story,' said Mr Carter. 'Yes,
it's certainly true. The Earl disappeared in the
year 1602 and he took all his treasure with him.
People have been looking for that treasure for
hundreds of years but it has never been found.'

The old house was an amazing place. Some of the
rooms were huge, others were tiny. There were stone
floors and window frames, and logs were piled up
in the fireplaces. The walls were covered with
old pictures, flags and armour. Most of the rooms
were very dark because the windows were quite small
and there were no electric lights.

When they had looked round the castle Mrs Patel
called the children into the Great Hall. 'I want
you to choose the most interesting thing you saw,
and draw it,' she said. 'I shall be coming round
to see how you are getting on.'

Hamid decided to draw a big bed. It was the
biggest bed he had ever seen. William remembered a
suit of armour he had seen in one of the smaller
rooms so he went off to draw that.

There was nobody in the little room. The suit of armour was standing beside the huge fireplace. There was a rather strange picture on the wall. 'That's funny,' thought William. 'There's nobody in that picture. It's just a blank space.'

He sat down and began to draw the armour.

Suddenly William shivered. 'It's gone cold in this room,' he thought. He looked at his drawing. Then he looked at the armour. He began to feel rather strange. The arm of the suit of armour had moved. As William watched, a small door began to open at the back of the fire-place. Out of the door came a little white dog.

'Hello,' said William. 'Where did you come from? How did you open that door? Was it you that moved the armour? Please, don't do it again. I'm trying to draw it.'

The dog barked, looked at William, and walked to
the door in the fire-place.

'Do you want to show me something?' asked William.
'Do you want me to follow you?' The dog wagged its
tail. William followed it through the door and
found himself in a dark passage. In the passage
were some stone steps. William went down the steps
and into a dark, damp tunnel. He could see light
behind a door at the end of it. The little dog
looked back to make sure that William was
following, and went through the door.

William tiptoed down the tunnel and looked round
the door. There was a little room with a candle
burning in an old candlestick. 'Somebody must be
down here,' thought William. 'Somebody must have
lit that candle.'

The little dog was standing by an old wooden
chest wagging its tail. 'I wonder if he wants me to
look into that chest,' thought William. 'Perhaps
it's full of dog biscuits. Or bones.'

12

William carried the candle over to the chest so
that he could see what he was doing. Then he tried
to lift the lid. It was very heavy but, at last,
he managed it.

The chest was full of treasure. There were gold
coins, diamonds and rubies as big as ping-pong
balls, pearl necklaces, gold plates and cups,
rings, and brooches. 'Wow!' gasped William.
'It's the old Earl's treasure!'

Suddenly, the dog barked. It made William jump
and drop the lid. Then he saw something else,
in the corner of the room.

It was a man dressed in strange clothes. He looked
at William and smiled.

'Oh no!' gasped William. 'It's the old Earl!'

'Good afternoon,' said the Earl.

'Goodbye!' said William. He grabbed the candle,
ran down the tunnel, up the steps, along the
passage, and through the door in the fire-place.

14

William was out of breath. 'Wait until Hamid hears about this,' he thought. He put the candle on a table and picked up his drawing. At that moment Mrs Patel and Mr Carter came into the room.

'Oh there you are, William,' she said. 'What have you been drawing? Let me see.'

'I started to draw that suit of armour,' explained William, 'but then a little white dog came through the door in the fire-place, so I followed him along the passage, down the stairs and into the tunnel. Then I found the room with the treasure and saw the ghost and . . .'

15

'Wait a minute! Slow down!' said Mrs Patel. 'What an imagination you have, William! What's all this about a dog, and a door in the fire-place?'

William looked at the fire-place but the door had closed again. There was no way through.

'There was a door!' said William. 'And a little dog, and treasure and a ghost! I know there was!'

Mrs Patel smiled. 'It sounds like a very good story,' she said. 'I hope you'll write it all down when we go back to school.'

'Look!' said William, pointing at the picture. 'It's them! That's the man I met in the room, and that's his little white dog. There was nobody in that picture when I first looked at it.'

Mr Carter laughed. 'Well, it's true that it's a picture of the Earl and his dog. But that painting has been like that since it was painted, hundreds of years ago. You've been dreaming, William.'

'But I wasn't! I know I wasn't!' said William. 'What about the treasure? Don't you want to find it?'

Mr Carter looked at the back of the fire-place. 'I'm afraid this looks solid to me. I can't see anything that looks like a door,' he said.

On the way back to school, William told Hamid about
his adventure. 'It really did happen,' he said. 'I
met the man in the picture and his dog, but nobody
will believe me.'

'That's what happens with ghost stories,' said
Hamid. 'Nobody ever believes them. Perhaps you did
just fall asleep and dream it all.'

'Well, perhaps I did,' agreed William. 'But it
seemed real at the time. At least it will make a
good story when I have to write about Gloomy Castle.'

18

All about ghosts

There are no such things as ghosts but, since earliest times, people have told or written ghost stories. Perhaps this is because people want to believe in them. Perhaps it's because we like to frighten each other.

Even today people like to read about ghosts.
There are often stories in the newspapers about
families who have been haunted. There are also
plenty of books and films about ghosts and haunted
houses. Every castle, inn, or theatre seems to
have at least one ghost and some have dozens.
Most of the ghost stories people tell seem to use
the same ideas over and over again. It's not easy
to think up a new sort of ghost story. You might
like to try yourself.

A traditional ghost story

There are many ghost stories like this one. This is about a teacher who is going to spend her holidays with her sister who lives in the country.

Miss Terry's holiday

Miss Terry was on holiday. She was going to visit her sister in Devon. She put two big suitcases in the boot of her car and made herself some egg sandwiches and a flask of coffee. 'What a fantastic, sunny day,' she thought. 'As soon as I get off the motorway, I'll stop for a picnic.'

By lunchtime she was in the Devon countryside. She had almost reached her sister's house. 'I wonder if I should forget about the picnic,' she thought. 'After all, I'm almost there.'

She drove along the narrow lanes in the shade of the tall hedgerows. Suddenly she saw something which made her stop the car. On the side of a hill was a beautiful meadow. There were tall oak trees and a little stream. 'That's a good place for a picnic,' thought Miss Terry.

She parked her car, found her flask and sandwiches and climbed over the gate into the meadow.

The best place to sit was under one of the trees.
As she ate her sandwiches she watched a pair of
kingfishers diving into the stream. In the
distance she could see the thatched roof of a
cottage. Behind it the hills rose gently up towards
the moor. 'What a beautiful spot,' thought Miss
Terry. 'I could stay here all day.' She closed her
eyes and a few moments later she was asleep.

The rain woke her up. While she had been asleep
the sky had turned grey. The birds had stopped
singing and there was a strange chill in the air.
'Oh no!' said Miss Terry. 'I knew it was too good
to last,' and she ran to her car.

Lightning flashed in the darkening sky and thunder rolled up and down the valley. 'Just made it!' gasped Miss Terry as the heavy rain began to pound down on the roof of her car.

There was worse to come. The car refused to start. 'Just my luck,' thought Miss Terry. 'First my picnic is spoilt, and now I'm going to get soaked.' She opened the bonnet of her car and tried to start it. After a few minutes she was wet through but she couldn't start her car. 'I'll have to run down to that cottage, and phone a garage,' she thought.

She knocked at the door of the cottage but for a long time nobody came. She opened the door and shouted. 'Hello. Is anybody here?'

'I'm here,' said a little girl, 'and so is my grandmother. Why don't you come inside and get dry?'

'Thank you,' said Miss Terry. 'That's very kind of you. My car has broken down and I must get help. Is there a garage in the next village?' The little girl didn't answer. She just smiled and led the way into the kitchen.

The kitchen was very neat and tidy with a lot of old-fashioned things in it. Miss Terry noticed there was no electric kettle, no fridge, no mixer and nothing made of plastic. There was an old-fashioned stove built into the fire-place. Over the big wooden table hung an oil lamp.

'The old lady must have lived here all her life,' thought Miss Terry. 'I expect she doesn't like modern things.'

'Grannie will be home soon,' smiled the little girl. She made this cake before she went out. Would you like a piece?' The cake was on the wooden table. It had not long been out of the oven. Its delicious smell filled the kitchen.

'That's very kind of you,' said Miss Terry, 'but won't your grandmother mind?'

'Oh no,' said the girl. 'I'm sure she'd like you to try it. Grannie is very proud of her cakes.'

She cut two slices of the cake and gave one to Miss Terry. It was one of the most delicious cakes Miss Terry had ever tasted.

'Would you like another slice?' asked the little girl.

'No thank you,' said Miss Terry. 'I really must see about getting the car repaired. Do you know where the nearest garage is?' The little girl looked puzzled. She didn't seem to understand.

'Well, is there a phone here?' asked Miss Terry.

'I don't know what a phone is,' said the girl.

Miss Terry was amazed. 'You must know what a telephone is!' she gasped. The little girl smiled and shook her head.

'It's stopped raining now,' she said. 'I could show you the short cut to the village. You'll get help there. It's not very far.'

So they went out of the cottage and walked along the banks of the stream. They crossed a muddy field and came out into the narrow lane that led down into the village. 'There it is,' said the little girl. 'I can't come any further because my Grannie will be home soon, and she will wonder where I am.'

Miss Terry thanked her for the cake and for her help and walked down to the village alone.

There was a garage in the village. Miss Terry told the mechanic about her car.

'Jump in the van,' he said. 'You can show me where your car is.' They drove out of the village and up the hill.

It was quite a while before the mechanic could start the car. While he was working Miss Terry told him about the little girl and her Grandmother. He looked thoughtful and rather puzzled. 'Nobody lives along this lane that I know of,' he said. 'There's only one cottage out here and that's been in ruins for the past sixty years.' 'That can't be true,' said Miss Terry. 'I was in the cottage only half an hour ago.'

When the mechanic had finished his work and driven away, Miss Terry got into her car. She went down the hill to the cottage.

Only the walls were standing. The neatly thatched roof had disappeared and a broken door swung on its rusty hinges. There was no glass in the windows and the well-kept garden was a tangle of weeds.

Miss Terry pulled open the broken door and went into the ruined kitchen. As she looked at the remains of an old wooden table she thought she heard the little girl's voice whisper 'Goodbye.'